For Hannah and Andy, who always remember.

Copyright © 1991 Ruth Gembicki Bragg.
Published by Picture Book Studio, Saxonville, MA.
Distributed in Canada by Vanwell Publishing, St. Catharines, Ont.
All rights reserved.
Printed in Hong Kong.
10 9 8 7 6 5 4 3 2 1

Library of Congress Cataloging in Publication Data
Bragg, Ruth
The Birthday Bears / illustrated by Ruth Gembicki Bragg.
Summary: Greedy bears disrupt a birthday dinner, grunting in the gravy
and threatening to eat the human celebrants for dessert.
ISBN 0-88708-139-8
[1. Bears–Fiction. 2. Birthdays–Fiction.] I. Title.
PZ7.B7335Bi 1990
[E]–dc20   90-7385

Ask your bookseller for **Mrs. Muggle's Sparkle**,
another Picture Book Studio book by Ruth Bragg.

The Birthday Bears

RUTH GEMBICKI BRAGG

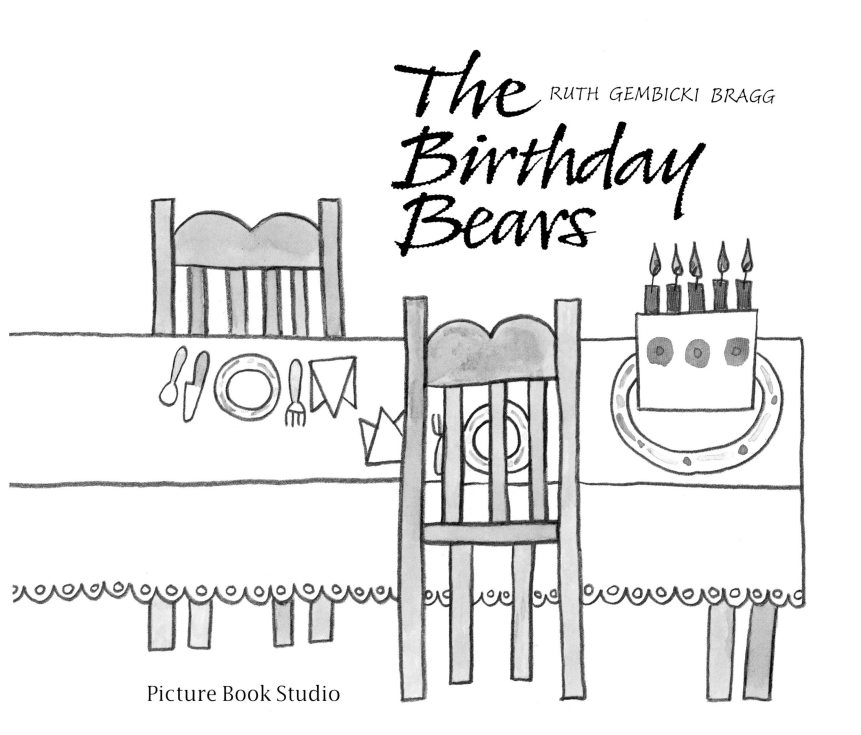

Picture Book Studio

Remember? Do you remember?
It was on your birthday a year ago.

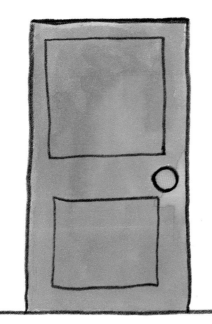

We had spaghetti and mashed potatoes and peas for dinner, and applesauce too. And chocolate cake with roses, your favorite. And even ice cream, three different flavors, for dessert. Remember that?

And we had just started our cake with roses when the doorbell rang…

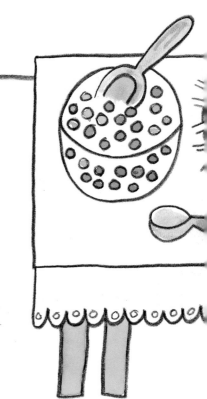

…and the bears came striding in!

Big bears, little bears, kodiaks and grizzlies, mamas and papas and babies and toddler bears, great gray grumpy grandparent bears. How many bears? Too many! One bear is too many if you didn't invite it to come. Did you invite them? If you did, you forgot to tell me why.

Sniffling, snuffling, they marched right up to the table like they owned the place. They ate all the peas and all the potatoes. They grunted in the gravy, and lapped up all of the applesauce. They ate all the spaghetti! All of it! Oh, what bears! I never will ever forget.

They wiped their sticky mouths on their sleeves.
They wiped their terrible paws on the tablecloth.
They burped and didn't say, "Excuse me."
They smacked their smeary lips like this: "smack! smack! **SMACK!**"

They made rude remarks about the
food and grabbed and growled
and grumbled, sticking out their
greedy tongues, poking each
other with their gooey elbows.
They giggled as they gobbled
at the laces of our shoes.

We were *their* dessert!
What did we do? What could we do? We did what we could.
And what was that? Do you remember? I remember.
I will never, never, never forget. We jumped onto the table!

And just as the biggest, grizzliest, grumpiest, growliest, hungriest bear
with the longest, sharpest claws and the shiniest, whitest teeth
was lifting its little child up to take a bite, a very toothy bite,
of your very best, most tender, favorite toe…

We screeched like fire trucks!
EEEoooEEEoooEEEooo!
We howled like sirens!
OOOeeeOOOeeeOOOeee!

The Police came! with whistles!
TWEE! TWEE! TWEE! TWEE!

And the Zoo Keepers came! with nets!
"Stop that! Right now!" they shouted
and waved their nets at the bears.

And the Newspaper People came with cameras.
POW! flashed their lights.

Now the *bears* were the ones who were so, so afraid.

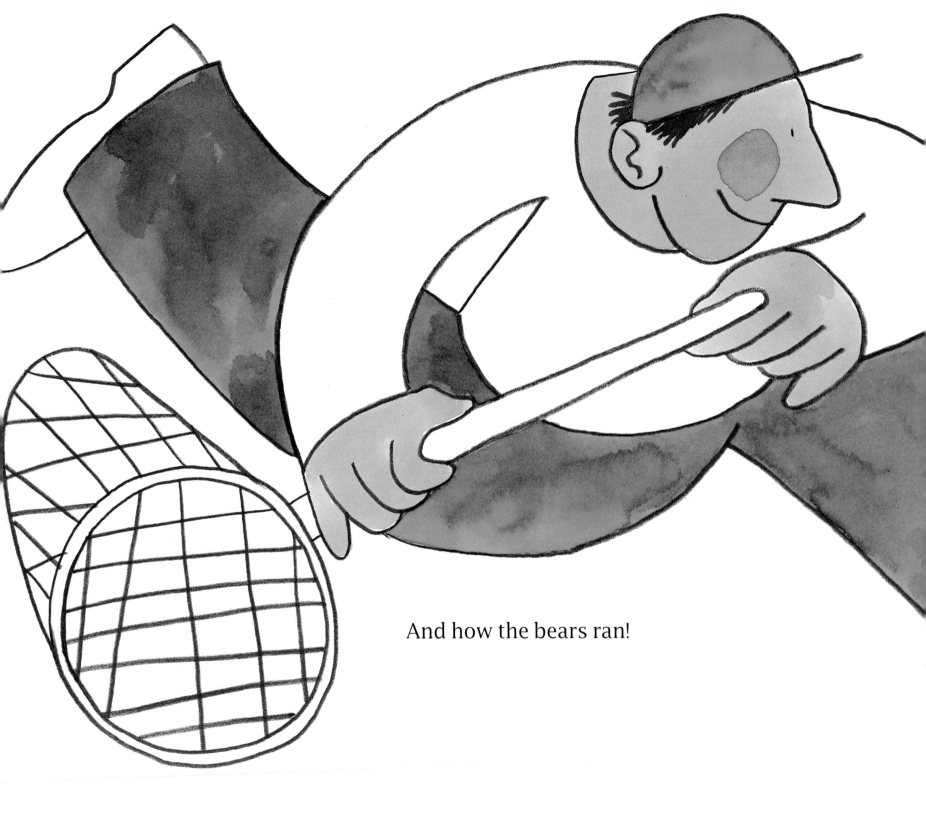

And how the bears ran!

One ran out of the front door,
two slid out of the back,
three jumped out of a window,
and four tried to drive away in a run-down, beat-up pickup truck.

Remember that? Remember?
I remember it all as if it had happened yesterday.

The Police and the Zoo Keepers captured the bears.
With our help, not one bear got away.

The Chief of Police gave us medals for being so smart. The Chief of the Zoo Keepers gave us rewards for being so brave. And the Newspaper People took our pictures because we were so wonderful. Remember that? You stood right next to the polar bear with frosting on its chin.

What a day!

Finally, the Police and the Chief of Police,
the Zoo Keepers and the Chief of the Zoo Keepers,
the Newspaper People and the bears said goodbye.

And we sat down again to have ice cream,
three different flavors, in peace and quiet,
just like today. Remember? Do you remember?
It was on your birthday a year ago. Well…

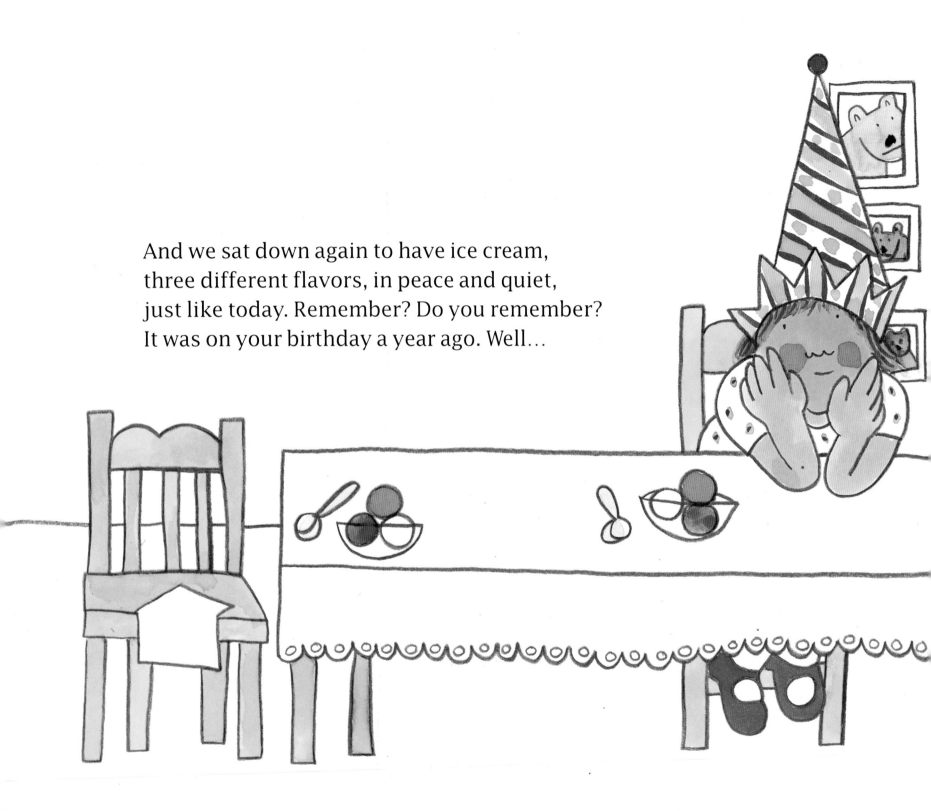

You remember, I remember, and guess what?...

The bears remember too!